This book

belongs to

WITHDRAWN

D0178302

WITHDRAWN FOR SALE

GULLANE

9931044977

For Paul
C.F.

For Joseph Thompson with love
K.S.

GLOUCESTERSHIRE COUNTY LIBRARY

9931044977	
PETERS	02-Oct-07
	£5.99

First published in 2006 in Great Britain by Gullane Children's Books
This paperback edition published in 2007 by
Gullane Children's Books
an imprint of Pinwheel Limited
Winchester House, 259-269 Old Marylebone Road,
London NW1 5XJ

1 3 5 7 9 10 8 6 4 2

Text © Claire Freedman 2006
Illustrations © Kristina Stephenson 2006

The right of Claire Freedman and Kristina Stephenson to be identified as the author and illustrator of this work
has been asserted by them in accordance with the Copyright, Designs, and Patents Act, 1988.
A CIP record for this title is available from the British Library.

ISBN-13: 978-1-86233-593-6
ISBN-10: 1-86233-593-1

All rights reserved. No part of this publication may be reproduced,
stored in a retrieval system, or transmitted in any form or by any means,
electronic, mechanical, photocopying, recording or otherwise, without prior permission.

Printed and bound in China

New Kid In Town

Claire Freedman
Kristina Stephenson

GULLANE
CHILDREN'S BOOKS

Mouse was the New Kid In Town. He bounced in from over the hill, looking for a new place to live, and came upon Badger's Bakery. "Hello!" said Mouse, strolling in. "I'm the New Kid In Town!"

"Welcome!" Badger replied. "You'll love living in our town. It's the best place for apricot muffins!" "But," Badger added, "watch out for the nasty Big Wolf who lives on the hill. He's huge and hairy, and wild and scary! **BEWARE!**"

Mouse bought some apricot muffins to eat in
the park. Giraffe came and sat next to him.
"Hello!" said Giraffe. "So you're
the New Kid In Town?"
"Yes!" said Mouse.

"This is a very friendly place," said Giraffe. "But," she whispered, "**BEWARE** of the horrible Big Wolf who lives on the hill. He's ugly and mean, and his teeth are slime green! Watch out!"

That afternoon, Mouse was admiring a very pretty
empty cottage, when Donkey came along.
"You must be the New Kid In Town!" said Donkey.
"That's me!" said Mouse.
"Have you visited our skating rink yet?"
asked Donkey. "We have competitions
with exciting prizes!"

"I love skating," cried Mouse.
"Come along, then," whispered Donkey.
"But keep an eye out for the horrible Big Wolf.
His jaws go **KER-RUNCH**, and he'll
eat you for lunch! Take care!"

The following morning, Mouse moved
his belongings into the pretty cottage.
He swept and dusted, unpacked and tidied.
Soon everything was spick and span.

Mouse folded up his apron.
"Perfect!" he smiled. "Just
one thing needs sorting out!"

Mouse marched out, past Badger's Bakery, through
the park, alongside the skating rink and up the hill . . .
the hill where Big Wolf lived!
"I'm not scared of the Big Bad Wolf!" he sang.
Mouse had only taken a few more steps when . . .

"Grrrrrrgh!"

He heard
a horrible,
horrible noise!
And, suddenly,
out sprang . . .

Big
Wolf!

"Who are you?" snarled Big Wolf.
"I'm the New Kid In Town!" said Mouse.
"Perhaps you haven't heard about me, yet!" Big Wolf laughed.
"I'm big and I'm hairy, I'm wild and I'm scary!"

"I think you look rather smart and neat!" smiled Mouse. "What a nice thing to say!" replied Big Wolf shyly. "No one's ever paid me a compliment before!"

Then, suddenly, Big Wolf frowned.
"You think I'm ugly and mean, because my
teeth are slime green – don't you?" Big Wolf growled.
Mouse shook his head. "Ugly? Not with that cheerful smile,"
he said. "I'm sure you're not mean either."

"I'm not!" said Big Wolf, really smiling now.
"And my teeth are only green from chewing grass!"
"I could lend you a toothbrush!" Mouse offered.
"So kind!" said Big Wolf.

"But my big jaws go KER-RUNCH. Aren't you scared I'll eat you for lunch?!"
"You wouldn't eat me!" Mouse replied. "Not now we've become such good friends!"

"Whaaaah!
Whaaaaaah!"

Big Wolf sobbed loudly
on Mouse's shoulder.
"I've never had a friend
before!" he howled.
"There, there!" said Mouse.
"Blow your nose on this. Then
come back to town with me!"

"But I can't come to town with you," said Wolf.
"Why not?" asked Mouse.
"Because . . . I'm scared!" sniffed Big Wolf.
"They all hate me down there!"
"Bye then!" waved Mouse.

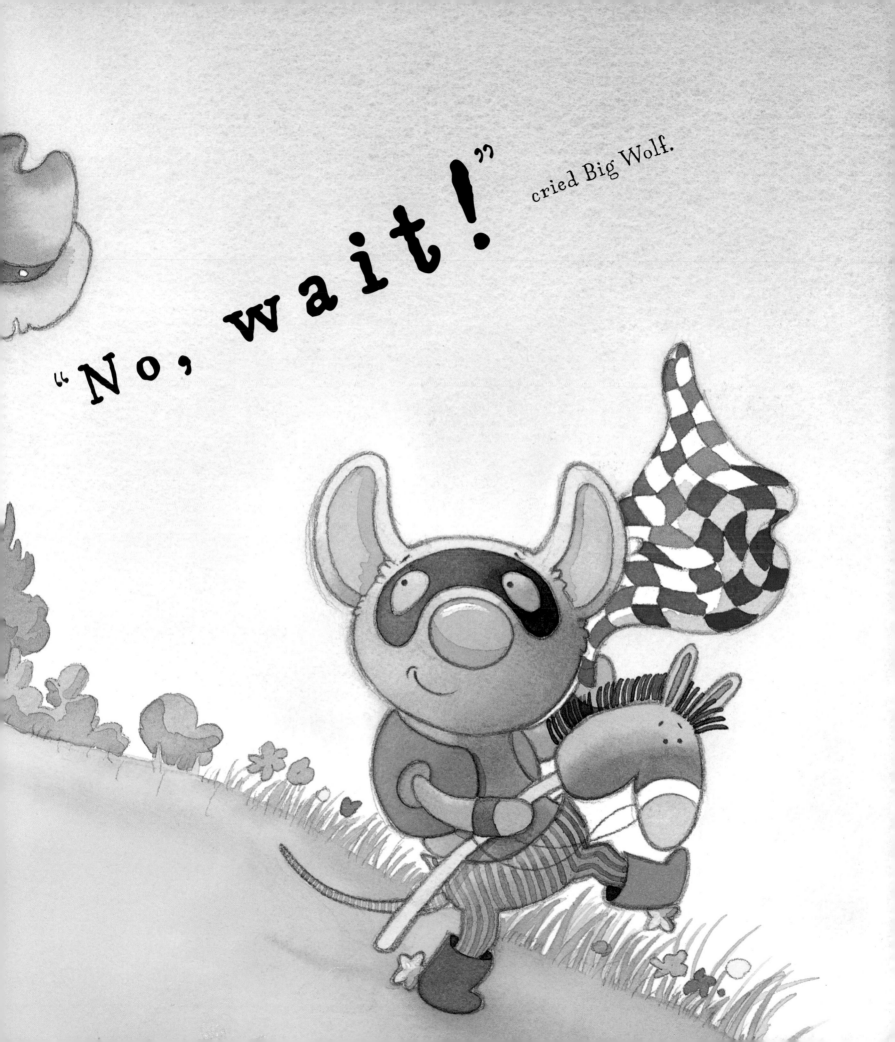

At the bottom of the hill, Mouse could see Badger, Giraffe and Donkey waiting anxiously. "Yooo-Hooo!" waved Mouse cheerily. "Come and meet Big Wolf. He'd like to come and live with us all!" **"Not likely!"** said Badger. **"You're joking!"** gasped Donkey. "**Help!**" cried Giraffe.

"See!" said Big Wolf. "No one wants me!"
He burst into floods of tears again.
"Don't worry!" Mouse told him. "I'll soon sort this out!"

"Come on, everyone!" Mouse said.
"Big Wolf may look wild and scary,
but it's not his fault he's hairy!
And although his eyes are yellow,
he's a friendly kind of fellow!"

"Hmm," said Badger, "I suppose he's never really done anyone any harm." "That's true!" said Giraffe and Donkey. "Maybe we could give him a chance!"

Suddenly Big Wolf's tummy rumbled very loudly!
"Oh dear, I don't like the sound of that!" said Donkey in a scared voice.
"N e i t h e r d o w e . . ." trembled the others.

"GGGRRR!"

"I'm **STARVING!**" Big Wolf said.
"I could just fancy a tasty . . ."

". . .BAKED BADGER?" gulped Badger.

". . . GRILLED GIRAFFE?"
gasped Giraffe.

". . . B-B-BUTTERED
DONKEY?" stuttered Donkey.

"Surely not . . .
MOUSE MOUSSE?" giggled Mouse.

"Yuk, and Double YUK!" laughed Big Wolf.
"I was thinking of apricot muffins!"
"HOORAH!" chorused Badger,
Giraffe, Donkey and Mouse.
"Apricot muffins it is then –
as many as you like!

After all, you are
going to be the . . .

NEW KID IN TOWN!"

Other Gullane Children's Books for you to enjoy...

Little Lion Lost!
MARK MARSHALL

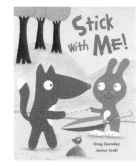

Stick with Me!
GREG GORMLEY •
JAMES CROFT

The Lamb-a-roo
DIANA KIMPTON • ROSALIND BEARDSHAW